A New Task

The Little Angel of Friendship jumped to his feet. "Have you got a job for me?" he asked.

"You're certainly the eager one," said the archangel.

"I only need a handful of feathers and I'll earn my wings and become an archangel, like you." The Little Angel of Friendship hopped on one foot all around the archangel. He landed in front of her and threw his hands out to both sides. "Ta-da! The almost-archangel of friendship stands before you ready for the tallest task."

Aladdin

Angelwings

№ 1

Friends
Everywhere

Donna Jo Napoli

illustrations by Lauren Klementz-Harte

Aladdin Paperbacks

*Thank you to my family, Brenda Bowen,
Doreen Deluca, and Richard Tchen*

First Aladdin Paperbacks edition October 1999

Text copyright © 1999 by Donna Jo Napoli
Illustrations copyright © 1999 by Lauren Klementz-Harte

Aladdin Paperbacks
An imprint of Simon & Schuster Children's Division
1230 Avenue of the Americas
New York, NY 10020

Designed by Steve Scott
The text for this book was set in Minister Light and Cheltenham.
The illustrations were rendered in ink and wash.
Printed and bound in the United States of America
10 9 8 7 6 5 4 3 2

Library of Congress Cataloging-in-Publication Data
Napoli, Donna Jo, 1948–
Friends everywhere / Donna Jo Napoli. — 1st Aladdin Paperbacks ed.
p.   cm. — (Aladdin Angelwings ; 1)
Summary: The Little Angel of Friendship watches over Patricia,
a nine-year-old deaf girl, as she moves from the family farm to the city
and tries to make friends with hearing people.
ISBN 0-689-82694-X (pbk.)
[1. Angels—Fiction. 2. Deaf—Fiction. 3. Physically handicapped—
Fiction. 4. Moving, Household—Fiction. 5. Friendship—Fiction.]
I. Title. II. Series: Napoli, Donna Jo, 1948–   Aladdin Angelwings ; 1.
PZ7.N15Fr   1999
[Fic]—dc21   98-52882
CIP   AC

*This whole series is dedicated to Brenda Bowen,
the best angel a writer could have*

Friends
Everywhere

Angel Talk

The Little Angel of Friendship sat with his arms clasped around his knees. "Any minute now," he whispered. "I can't wait."

"Take a deep breath," said the little angel at his side. "Like me. It helps." She took a deep breath.

All the little angels sucked in their breath in unison.

The Little Angel of Friendship breathed into the very bottom of his lungs. He let the air out slowly. And, oh, yes, here came the first rays of morning's light over the horizon. "This is the best time of day."

"The very best," murmured a little angel in front of him.

"Little Angel of Friendship, is that you?"

1

The Archangel of Friendship came up behind the group of little angels. "Good morning, all of you."

The little angels smiled.

The Little Angel of Friendship jumped to his feet. "Have you got a job for me?" He wove his way out to the edge of the little angels.

"You're certainly the eager one," said the archangel.

"I only need a handful of feathers and I'll earn my wings and become an archangel, like you." The Little Angel of Friendship hopped on one foot all around the archangel. He landed in front of her and threw his hands out to both sides. "Ta-da! The almost-archangel of friendship stands before you ready for the tallest task."

The little angels laughed.

"It's a tall task, all right," said the archangel. "And I think it'll be easier if we start right away, so you can follow her through her day."

"Bye, everyone," called the Little Angel of

Friendship. He fell into step beside the archangel. "Who is she?"

"Patricia."

"And what's her problem?"

"Hi," called a little angel racing by toward the group of little angels. "Am I too late for all the fun?"

"Too late for the sunrise, but never too late for all the fun," said the Little Angel of Friendship.

"Hi," called another little angel, kneeling over a fire. "I'm going to make a wonderful country breakfast. Aren't you going to have some?"

"Another day," said the Little Angel of Friendship. "But it smells great."

"Hey," called a third little angel. "Doesn't my gown shine like the sun? I just washed it."

"Almost like the sun," said the Little Angel of Friendship. They walked on.

"Everyone knows you. You must be the most popular little angel of all," said the Archangel of Friendship.

"Probably," said the Little Angel of Friendship.

"Yo," called a little angel looking up from a pad of paper.

The Little Angel of Friendship gave a quick wave.

The other little angel kept wandering along, scribbling on his paper, then looking up vaguely, then scribbling again.

"You hardly gave him any notice at all," said the archangel.

"No one really likes him," said the Little Angel of Friendship.

"How come?"

"They say he's a nerd—always reading or writing. A bore."

"Is he?"

"How should I know? I don't know him. He never says anything more than 'yo' to me." The Little Angel of Friendship walked fast. "Tell me about her—about Patricia. What's her problem?"

"You'll see soon enough."

The little angel smiled to himself. He'd been hoping for a hard task soon, and here it was. A task hard enough to be worth several feathers, enough to complete his wings. Every time a little angel earned wings, a bell rang. The Little Angel of Friendship imagined the loud ring that would announce his earning his wings. His body trembled with the reverberation of the huge bell.

The Last Day

Patricia sat in the ash tree with her legs straddling the rough branch. She looked out over the cornfields. The morning was still cool, but she knew already that it would be a hot day.

Wind gently stirred the leaves around her. The tips of the cornstalks fluttered. Patrica put her hands on the branch under her bottom and pushed her face forward into the breeze. Curls escaped from her ponytail and tickled her ears.

Dad wasn't in the fields, though the sun was fully up. He was probably back at the house helping Mom with the last-minute packing. They were moving tomorrow. Leaving the farm to Grandpa and Uncle Rhoads.

Leaving the cornfields.

The tree shook just the smallest bit. Patricia looked down. Sure enough, Nanny butted the trunk again. Patricia climbed to the ground and scratched the goat behind her stiff ears. Nanny didn't know they were leaving. Nanny didn't know much. Patricia hugged the goat around the neck, pulling on the bell that hung there. Nanny twisted and jumped away, ready for play.

Patricia ran to the big barrel by the barn. Once that barrel had held fifty-five gallons of machine oil. But that was years ago. Now it lay on its side smelling of nothing but the earth around it. It was another of Patricia's favorite spots. She climbed in and waited in a squat. Nanny knocked against it hard and rolled her. Patricia laughed and laughed.

When she crawled out of the barrel, Grandpa stood waiting for her. He led her toward the garage. Nanny followed till Grandpa chased her off. In the driveway stood a girl's bike with training wheels. It wasn't a new bike, but Patricia never had seen it before.

Patricia looked at Grandpa with a question on her face.

"You'll need a bike. All the city kids ride bikes."

Patricia shook her head. "Mom told me I'll never be able to ride a bike. I don't have the balance."

"That's why I put on these extra wheels."

"Kids my age don't use training wheels."

"They're not training wheels for you. They're balance wheels." Grandpa smiled. "Get on and ride."

Patricia shook her head again. Training wheels—one more way she'd be different from everyone else. "I'd rather walk everywhere."

"Walking is slow."

"I don't like to rush."

"All right." Grandpa rubbed a cloth over the handlebars. "Just take the bike with you.

If you don't use it, that's okay. And who knows? You might."

"Maybe I shouldn't go, Grandpa. Maybe I should stay here on the farm with you and Uncle Rhoads."

"We've been through this." Grandpa hung the cloth on a hook. "It's a good move. You'll be able to see friends every day when you live in the city, instead of just in school, like now."

"If I have friends."

"You'll have friends. Everybody's going to love you." Grandpa put on his earplugs. "I'm going haying at the Websters'. Want to come?"

Patricia followed Grandpa out to the tractor. The baler was already attached to the back. She got up onto the high seat beside him. She didn't need earplugs; the tremendous noise didn't bother her. In fact, she loved the rumble that came up through the engine and made the seat shake under her.

"Maybe I can stay here with you just for the rest of the summer."

But Grandpa's hands were busy with driving, and his eyes were on the road ahead.

This was the last time Patricia would climb the ash tree. The last time Nanny would roll her in the barrel. The last time she'd ride the tractor with Grandpa. The last time for who knows how long.

Patricia's fingers curled tight over the front edge of her seat.

Angel Talk

She's scared," said the Little Angel of Friendship.

"Wouldn't you be?" said the archangel.

"The house looks big and well-kept up. The fields are growing. It seems like the family has a good life here. Why are they moving?"

The Archangel of Friendship smiled. "You act like Patrica. She's been begging her father for the past month not to go."

"So why are they going?"

"Her father got a good job offer. He's been going to a technical night school. It's time for a change—that's what he thinks." The archangel pressed the middle knuckles of her left fingers between the thumb and index finger of her right hand. She went from finger to finger, worrying those knuckles.

The Little Angel of Friendship had spent a lot of time with this archangel. He knew that she did that to her fingers when she was particularly upset about a child. He understood; Patricia's situation made him anxious, too. "Will everyone really be different from her in their new place?"

"Well, she'll be in an ordinary neighborhood. And she'll go to an ordinary school."

"For the first time?"

"Yes," said the archangel. "Up till now she's gone to a special private school for deaf children."

"This is terrible," said the little angel. "How will she know what's going on?"

"She'll have Beth Anne, her own special helper. Beth Anne will interpret for her." The archangel rubbed her knuckles. "But other than that, she'll be surrounded by people she doesn't understand. Patricia has always lived out here on the farm with her family."

"But she must have some skills at making

friends. She must have made friends at her school," said the little angel.

"Oh, yes. She has plenty of friends there. In fact, she's a lot like you—she's always been popular."

"Up to now," said the Little Angel of Friendship softly.

"Up to now."

"Wow," said the little angel. "You've given me the hardest task I've ever had."

"Are you scared?"

"Wouldn't you be?" asked the little angel.

The archangel smiled. "So we're back to where we started."

The Little Angel of Friendship squared his shoulders. "I guess that means it's time to begin."

Moving

After dinner, Patricia went to her room with Dad and Mom. Three large empty boxes stood in a row. She looked at her parents.

Dad pointed. "This one is for your clothes. This one is for your books and toys. And this one is for everything else."

"What's everything else?"

"Whatever you want." Mom kissed Patricia on the cheek. "I put an outfit for tomorrow on the top of your bureau. Everything else gets packed."

"Isn't my bureau coming?"

"We've rented a furnished apartment at the start." Dad took a photograph out of his pocket. "Aunt Mary just got her film developed. She sent me this picture of the building."

Aunt Mary lived in the city and she had

found the apartment for them. Patricia looked at the building Dad pointed to now. It was surrounded by other buildings, with a snatch of grass out in front of some, and only two trees in the whole photo. Pathetic, scraggly things. Patricia loved climbing trees—she loved it so much that her name sign was the sign for "tree" using the hand shape of the alphabet letter P. "I'd never climb yucky trees like those. We'll have to change my name sign."

"You'll find good climbing trees. The city is full of parks."

Patricia's eyes went back to the apartment building itself. Four stories high and so wide. "It's huge."

Dad smiled. "The building is, but our apartment isn't. Later, when we know for sure what neighborhood we want to live in, we'll rent a bigger place and bring our own furniture."

"You mean we'll move again?"

"Not necessarily. That's why we chose this

building. If we like it there, they have lots of unfurnished apartments, too."

Mom put her hand on Patricia's shoulder and squeezed. "Do you need my help packing?"

Patricia shook her head.

"All right, then. I'll come back in an hour to see how you're doing."

Her parents left.

Patricia opened her top drawer and carefully moved the little stacks of neatly folded clothes to the first box. She did drawer after drawer, moving quickly. Then she went to the closet. She didn't know if she was supposed to take the clothes off the hangers first or not. But she didn't want to ask Mom. She wanted everything to be done by the time Mom came back. So she kept the hangers with the clothes and put each thing into the box, letting them fold back and forth accordion-style as she gently lowered them. She tucked her shoes into the corners. There was still plenty of room in the box, but that was all the clothes she had. So she bent down the four top flaps, one after the other, and tucked the tip of the last one under the first one, like she'd seen Mom do.

Patricia opened the large wooden toy box Grandpa had made for her. The metal teacups with the blue flowers painted on them sat one inside the other on top of the little saucers. The big dollies sat with the little ones in their laps. Everything was neatly arranged, just how she liked it. But everything would get jumbled in the box as they bumped along the road. Jumbled like her life. She scooped things up with both hands and dumped them in the moving box, helter-skelter. She scooped and scooped till the box was empty.

Then she sat on the floor, her chest heaving. She wanted to pound the floor with her fists, but if she did, she knew Mom would come running. And she didn't want Mom now.

She let herself fall onto her back, then she scootched herself along the floor till she was

completely under her bed. Her clothes were packed. Her toys were packed. And the third box stood waiting for whatever else she wanted. What else did she want?

Everything.

Patricia put her hands palms down on the floorboards and spread her fingers. The house was still. No water was running through the pipes. No one was walking in the living room or on the stairs. Probably they were all out on the porch. That's what they did on warm nights.

Where would they sit on warm nights in that huge apartment building?

And who would sit with them?

Who would sit with Patricia? Who would play with her ever?

Now she felt the running feet through the floorboards, running up the stairs, into her room. In an instant Mom slid across the floor and lay beside her. She laced her fingers through Patricia's.

Patricia swallowed the hurt in her throat. Mom was beside her now, and she had to admit it felt good.

But Mom couldn't stay beside her always. And she didn't want her to, anyway.

Patricia unlaced her fingers and kissed Mom on the cheek, just like Mom had kissed her earlier. They lay alone, side by side, under the bed.

Angel Talk

*I*t's amazing that her mother came up the stairs at just that moment," said the Archangel of Friendship, looking suspiciously at the little angel.

The little angel smiled. He took the archangel's hand and blew onto her palm.

The archangel pulled back, then rubbed her hands together to warm them. "You made me cold. Come hug me." Then she opened her mouth in realization. "Oh, is that what you did to her mother? Blow on her hand?"

"Yes. I figured it might give her a sense of how cold and lonely Patricia felt up there in her bedroom."

"I don't know if it did that, but I'm sure it made her need to get close to someone."

"Does Patricia lie under her bed often?" asked the little angel.

"Maybe not often, but whenever she's feeling particularly sad."

"And does her mother always crawl under the bed with her?"

The archangel nodded. "If she realizes Patricia is there, she does."

"What a strange family," said the little angel. "Do all deaf people do that?"

"Of course not. Every family has their own strange ways. But you went under that bed with her, right? Didn't you like it?"

"It was dark. And a little dusty."

"Is that all?" asked the archangel.

"Well, no. I guess it was nice, too. Sort of cozy."

"Exactly," said the archangel. "It's a comfort."

The Little Angel of Friendship remembered lying under the bed, looking up at the box springs. He gave himself a hug.

Lynsey

Moving in was fast, at least for Patricia. She threw everything from the first two boxes into her drawers. Her new bureau was larger than hers at the farm, even though her bedroom was smaller, so she used the bottom drawer for her toys. Later on, when she was done exploring, she'd take the time to put things away properly. And maybe then she'd open the third box.

Dad sat at a desk in the living room, organizing papers. Mom put dishes away in the kitchen cupboards. Patricia could watch both of them at once because the kitchen was separated from the living room by nothing but a counter.

The lights went on and off, on and off.

Mom looked at Dad. "Were you expecting someone?"

Dad shook his head.

Patricia answered the door.

A girl slightly taller than Patricia stood there and smiled. Then her mouth moved.

Patricia knew this would happen. Everyone but her own family moved their mouths like that. She'd seen them on visits into town. On TV. At the movies. Visitors to her school often moved their mouths like that, too. It was called speaking. People who did it were called hearing.

And now a hearing girl was speaking to Patricia. She stared at her face, at her funny lips and the way her cheeks tensed.

Dad came to the door and put his arm around Patricia. He moved his mouth.

The girl looked at Dad, then she looked at Patricia. Then she moved her mouth at Dad again.

"She lives across the hall." Dad pointed at the door to the girl's apartment. "She goes to the same school you'll be going to. And she wants to play. What do you think?"

"What's her name?"

Dad moved his mouth at the girl. The girl moved her mouth back.

Dad fingerspelled, "L-Y-N-S-E-Y."

Patricia pointed to herself, then finger-spelled to Lynsey, "P-A-T-R-I-C-I-A."

Lynsey looked at Dad.

Dad moved his mouth. He kept moving it.

Lynsey took Patricia by the hand and led her across the hall. Patricia wanted to look to Dad for reassurance, but she didn't want Lynsey to see her do it. She was big, after all. She shouldn't be needing her father's help. Anyway, there was nothing she needed help with. This would be okay. After all, it was just across the hall. If Patricia didn't like it, all she had to do was go home.

They went into Lynsey's living room. A boy who looked a lot like Lynsey stood with little barbells in his hands in front of the TV. He looked at them and moved his mouth. Lynsey moved her mouth back. Patricia smiled at the boy. He stared at her as though she were something truly odd. She stopped smiling, and her stomach lurched.

Lynsey pulled Patricia into a bedroom and shut the door behind them fast. She didn't look frightened, though. She was closing the boy out, not running away from him.

Lynsey opened a closet. Dolls and stuffed animals cluttered the floor—so many Barbies. Lynsey moved her mouth as she reached into the closet. She was speaking, but who was she speaking to? Lynsey handed Patricia a Barbie and grabbed one for herself. She sat down on the floor beside the bed and moved her mouth at Patricia. Then she patted the floor beside her, moving her hand up and down like in the sign for "ball." But there were no balls around. Lynsey moved her mouth again. She tugged on the leg of Patricia's shorts. She patted the floor. Her face showed frustration. She patted the floor again, more insistently this time.

Oh. She wanted Patricia to sit there. Of course. Patricia's face went hot. How stupid of her. She sat down where Lynsey had patted.

Lynsey walked her Barbie over to Patricia's and moved her mouth the whole time. Patricia looked at Lynsey. What kind of game were they playing? There was no point in signing to Lynsey; she didn't even know how to fingerspell, and Mom had told Patricia that when hearing people learn to sign, the first thing they learn is fingerspelling. So Lynsey didn't know the first thing. Patricia leaned toward Lynsey and lowered her eyebrows like she would if she was asking what they were doing.

Lynsey frowned. She moved her mouth. Then she took both Barbies and threw them into the closet. She put on a lady's hat and slung a purse over her shoulder.

Dress-up time? Patricia liked dress-up time. She got up and walked over behind Lynsey.

Lynsey ran out of the room.

Patricia ran after her.

Lynsey stood in the living room with a telephone to her ear. She moved her mouth and looked at Patricia and moved her mouth again. Patricia knew all about telephones. Grandpa and Uncle Rhoads used one, after all.

The boy was still in front of the TV, but now he stood on his head. He grinned at Patricia. Upside down like that, his grin looked like a scary, toothy frown. Patricia put her fingers in the corners of her mouth and pulled down so that it would look like a smile to the upside-down boy.

Lynsey hung up the phone and skipped over to the front door. She stuck her head out into the hall.

Patricia stood behind Lynsey and tried to see around her.

Another girl their age came running up. She moved her mouth and looked at Patricia. Her mouth moved and moved.

Patricia tried to smile

The girls pulled Patricia back into the bedroom. The other girl went straight to the closet. She seemed to know where everything was in that jumble, because within seconds she threw a scarf around her neck and was putting her feet into high heels.

Patricia loved wearing Mom's high heels. She pushed past Lynsey to look into the closet.

Lynsey pushed her back, moving her mouth. She stopped abruptly and rubbed her cheek, looking confused. Then she pressed hard on Patricia's shoulders with both hands.

Why? Patricia had to work to stay standing.

Lynsey pressed harder. Now the other girl pressed, too.

Patricia tried to fight them off.

They pressed hard.

Oh. They wanted her to sit again. Oh, how stupid she was being today. Okay. Patricia sat on the floor.

Lynsey shuffled through the mess in the

closet. She handed a string of pearls to the other girl and put a string of beads around her own neck. Then she pulled out a blanket and a pacifier. She put the blanket around Patricia's shoulders and tried to stuff the pacifier in her mouth.

Oh. Lynsey and the other girl were grown-ups, but Patricia was a baby. The grown-up women who spoke, and the baby who couldn't speak. Oh. Patricia pushed away the pacifier and stood up, letting the blanket fall on the floor behind her.

Lynsey shook her head and moved her mouth and tried to wrap Patricia up in the blanket again. She pressed on Patricia's shoulders and kept moving her mouth in the same way, over and over, her lips protruding just a little bit more each time, as though if she said something enough times, Patricia would finally understand. The other girl seemed to be saying the same thing Lynsey was saying.

Out of the corner of her eye, Patricia saw the door open. The boy's face peeked in, his eyes curious.

Patricia looked back at the girls, whose mouths were still doing the same motions. She couldn't stand to look at those mouths anymore. "I'm not a baby. And I'm not stupid."

Lynsey stared at Patricia's hands and arms as she signed. The other girl laughed.

Patricia ran past the boy, out through the living room, and across the hall into her new home.

And what a terrible new home it was.

Angel Talk

"It's all my fault," said the Little Angel of Friendship.

"What?" The Archangel of Friendship leaned over so that her face was level with his. "What's your fault?"

"Remember when Lynsey rubbed her cheek? That was because I blew on it. I thought it might make her realize how confused and left out Patricia felt. Instead, she got cold and ran for a blanket." The little angel balled his hands into fists and jammed them into his pockets. "If it weren't for me, Lynsey wouldn't have thought of playing grown-ups and baby."

"I don't know about that, little angel." The archangel pulled gently on the little angel's sleeve until he took that hand out of his pocket.

She held his hand. "Some girls love to play grown-ups and baby."

"Patricia doesn't."

"The day I first noticed her, she had dressed her goat up in a baby bonnet and was feeding it from a Yoo-Hoo bottle."

"Really?" The little angel laughed. He dropped the archangel's hand and ran ahead a little. "Did the goat like it?"

"You'd better believe it. Patricia mashed cookies in with the milk. The goat gobbled it up."

The little angel laughed again. Then he stopped and turned to the archangel. "But Patricia didn't like the game today."

"No." The archangel rubbed her knuckles.

"She thinks Lynsey and that other girl see her as stupid—like a baby."

The archangel rubbed her knuckles faster. "I know. I saw what she signed."

The little angel walked back to the archangel. "Patricia might just be acting sensitive because she's so scared by this move. Everybody acts a little jumpy sometimes." He slowly put one hand on the archangel's wrist as he looked up into her face and dared to say the words he hoped were wrong: "Or she might be right about those girls. I didn't think they looked very nice in the first place."

The archangel's face was as worried as the little angel had ever seen it.

Monkeys

Patricia tapped Dad on the shoulder.

Dad pulled his shoulders toward each other, arching backward. Then he sat up straighter at his computer. "Later," he signed. "I have to finish this before I go to work tomorrow."

Patricia tapped harder.

"Later!"

Patricia reached over and pressed the return button on the keyboard.

Dad looked at her, shocked. "What do you think you're doing? Don't you ever hit a key when I'm working. You could have messed up my work."

"I don't care."

"You'd better care. This job is important to all of us."

"Important to you. You. Not me. All you ever think about is you."

"What's on your mind?" Dad tried to pull Patricia onto his lap, but she held herself firm away from him. "What happened at that girl's house?"

"It's not a house. It's an apartment. We live in an apartment now. And I want our house."

"You'll get to like it here."

"You only say that because you can speak. You never let me learn to speak. You never let Mom learn to speak. You're mean, and I hate it here." Patricia ran to her room.

She crawled under her bed and lay on her back, her heart thumping. Patricia had never called Dad mean before. Dad was usually accused of being too softhearted. That's what Grandpa said, that Dad was too softhearted to own livestock. He'd never be able to slaughter them when it came time.

But now Patricia saw everything differently. Dad had moved them there because he'd gotten a job. And he'd gotten a job with these strange people who moved their mouths in such ugly ways because he could move his mouth that way, too. He could make friends.

Patricia would never make new friends here. Mom would come in soon and tell her to stop acting like this. But Patricia was right, and Mom was wrong.

Where was Mom, anyway? She must have been in the kitchen when Patricia came home. She must have seen Patricia call Dad mean. And if she hadn't, Dad would have told her by now. So where was she?

It smelled weird under this bed. Patricia sniffed hard. A plastic smell. The mattress must be new.

Patricia sidled out from under the bed and looked around the room. The bureau was new, too. And it didn't look like real wood. Her third box still sat in the corner, unopened. Everything in that box carried the smells of the farm. The smell of real things. If she opened it, maybe the room would seem more like home.

But she didn't want to like this room. She'd never open that box.

Mom came in. "Sit on the bed."

"I don't want to talk now."

Mom shook her head. "I wasn't asking you, I was ordering you." Her face was tight, and her eyes glittered. "Pay attention."

Patricia sat and looked at Mom.

"What did you study in your school?"

"You know. Everything. Math and reading and science and geography—everything."

"That's right." Mom sat down beside Patricia, facing her. "When I was your age, you know what I studied?"

"What?"

"How to speak. I couldn't hear anything. My ears are as deaf as yours. I spent my day—all day long—trying to copy the teacher. I had to feel her throat and cheeks and feel my own so I could copy hers. I had to

look in her mouth and then look in a mirror to see the inside of my own mouth. All day long, I tried to make the sounds she made."

"Could you do it?"

"No. Sometimes I'd get close. But almost never. And the whole time, I couldn't hear anything that was coming out of my mouth."

"Dad learned. He should have helped you."

"Dad was the best student in the school. But it was hard for him, too. Horribly hard. I remember him working like a crazy person. And, still, he didn't learn any real subjects until he was in high school. As for me, well, when I finished high school, I could barely read."

Patricia shook her head in disbelief. "Why?"

"We spent almost no time reading. Tell me, Patricia, what's Paris?"

"It's a big city in France. The capital."

"And where's France?"

"Across the Atlantic Ocean."

"And what pumps your blood?"

"My heart, of course."

"And what cleans your blood?"

"My kidneys, I think."

"I didn't know that when I was your age. We spent almost no time on geography or science. All we tried to do was learn to speak and to read lips—and that was impossible for many of us."

"Dad did it."

"Oh, Patricia. Some deaf people do learn to speak. But lots of others spend years trying to and never succeed. And even Dad hated going to the oral school. He thought it was like being one of those monkeys that people train to do tricks in a circus. We were all supposed to act like hearing people—but we're not. We're deaf. And so are you, Patricia."

"I want to hear."

"You can't. Everyone has things they can't do. You can't hear."

"I want to speak, then. Dad speaks. I want to, too."

"You could try for years and then you'd probably learn only well enough for the most patient people who see you all the time to understand you. And in the meantime, you wouldn't have the time to study anything else. You'd fall so far behind. Oh, Patricia, you have American Sign Language. You can express yourself fully. When I was a kid, we weren't even allowed to sign in our school because the teachers thought it would make us lazy about trying to learn to speak. So we were frustrated. All of us, locked inside our heads. I hated school."

Mom shut her eyes for a minute and shuddered. When she opened them, the glitter was gone. "I've been happy since I went to night school for reading classes. I've learned so many things. Things that you know already. You're getting a real education. And you're so good at reading and math that you can go to a school with any kind of kid and do just fine. It's the right time for us to make this move—you're ready, Patricia. And you're lucky. That little girl who lives across the hall probably only has one language. But you've got two. You use American Sign Language and you read and write English. You're lucky."

"I don't feel lucky; I can't make friends with Lynsey."

"I don't know whether you can make friends with this Lynsey girl or not. But you'll make friends. I'm sure of that. We'll go to all the activities of the deaf groups in the area. You'll have friends."

"Will there be other deaf kids at my school?"

"No. I'm sorry. The school is small."

"I want a friend at school, Mom. I want a friend at school."

Mom opened her arms, and Patricia crawled into the warm circle. She sat with her back against Mom's chest and watched

Mom's hands: "I bet you'll have a friend at school. You're just too wonderful—some-one's got to notice."

Patricia would go to her new school in just two weeks. It seemed like no time at all. She put her own hands on the backs of Mom's and made the sign over and over: "wonderful." But all she could think of was how the other girl had laughed when she'd signed.

Angel Talk

"I'm useless," said the Little Angel of Friendship.

"Why do you say that?"

"I can't begin to think of how to solve Patricia's problem. She can't speak. She can't hear. How can she ever make friends with ordinary kids?"

"Does every activity call for speaking?" asked the archangel.

"Well, no, of course not. But people can't learn about you without speaking."

"Really?" The Archangel of Friendship smiled. "There used to be a saying: 'Actions speak louder than words.'"

"You're right. People can get to know her and she can get to know them if only she can have the chance to do things with them without having to speak." The little angel hopped as high as he could. "Patricia's got to take every chance she gets to show them what kind of person she is. I can help her do that."

"Run with it," said the archangel. "Or, rather, hop with it."

Garbage

For the next week, Patricia managed not to think about Lynsey and the other girl during the day because Mom took her exploring the city while Dad went to work. And the city was amazing—so many stores and restaurants and movie theaters and parks and museums. It was overwhelming sometimes, but in an exhilarating way.

But at night the memory returned—the memory of how bad things had gone with Lynsey and the other girl. So every night Patricia sat in front of the TV and tried to read the characters' lips. She would read the closed captions, which printed out what the characters were saying, and then study their lips.

At first it seemed that some words were easy. Like "mom." The lips came together at the beginning and at the end. But just when she thought she could recognize "mom," she found out that "Bob" looked the same—not just alike, but truly the same. And when she watched the news, she found out that "mob" and "bomb" looked the same as them, too. And almost every word had problems like that. So many words looked the same that Patricia couldn't understand anything. Nothing. It didn't make sense.

By Thursday night, Patricia was convinced that lip-reading was hard, after all. But Mom kept promising that this Sunday they'd go to a picnic for deaf people. So Patricia would find someone to play with there. It didn't matter if she wouldn't have friends in school, as long as she had friends somewhere.

After dinner on Friday, Mom asked Patricia to carry the garbage out to the back of the apartment building. Patricia took the rear stairs and went outside to the Dumpster. Lynsey and the boy Patricia figured must be her twin brother were standing in the tiny backyard moving their mouths at each other and looking angry. Patricia stood there and watched them. She prepared to smile as sweetly as she knew how.

Lynsey held up a bald Barbie doll and waved it in front of the boy's face and moved her mouth faster. Soon she would look Patricia's way.

Patricia smiled now, as wide as she could.

Lynsey stamped her foot and ran inside, without so much as a glance at Patricia.

Patricia felt like she'd been slapped. It was much worse than if Lynsey had moved her mouth at her, no matter what Lynsey said. Being ignored was much, much worse. She blinked to keep back tears.

The boy was looking at her.

Patricia wanted to run away. But she hadn't done anything wrong. They had no right to make her feel this way. She stood her ground and looked right back at him.

He came up to her, took the garbage bag from her hands, and threw it into the Dumpster. Then he went over to the bushes in the corner of the yard and pulled out a big green plastic garbage can, like the type Patricia had back on the farm. He pried off the lid and reached inside. Next he ran to a faucet on the side of the building and turned it on. He kept his back to Patricia. Suddenly, he threw something to her.

She caught it automatically. It was a squirt gun. And it was full.

The boy held an identical squirt gun in his hand. He grinned fiendishly, squirted her, and jumped behind the garbage can.

Patricia was so surprised, she just stood there and wiped the water from her face.

The boy leaned out and squirted her in the chest.

Whoa. This was war! Patricia squirted back, but the boy was behind the garbage can again. She saw him coming out for another

round, so she quickly shot at him and squeezed herself behind the big Dumpster.

The boy's face appeared at the corner of the Dumpster. He shot.

She shot back and worked her way along the back of the Dumpster and out the other side, the two of them shooting at each other the whole time. She came around to the front of the Dumpster and looked around for new cover. But this yard was pathetic—there was nowhere to hide.

The boy appeared at the other corner of the Dumpster. He squirted, but he was out of water.

Patricia squirted back till her gun was empty. She raised it over her head in triumph.

The boy ran back to the green garbage can and leaned halfway into it.

Patricia followed him and looked over his shoulder. The can was full of all kinds of balls and a jump rope and a baseball bat and who knew what else. Patricia wasn't really good at throwing and catching. But she could get good. If this boy wanted to play, she'd give it a try.

A breeze came up out of nowhere. It blew Patricia's hair back off her temples. She felt like she was on the farm again, in the ash tree, with Nanny banging her head against the trunk down below. A sudden urge made her tap the boy on the back.

He straightened up and looked at her inquisitively.

Patricia grabbed the garbage can in a bear hug, picked it up, and dumped everything out of it.

The boy stared at her.

She grinned at him, the same way he had grinned at her. Then she put the garbage can on its side and motioned for him to get in.

The boy looked skeptical, but he crawled into the garbage can.

Patricia rolled him over and over in the grass. She could feel the reverberations of his laughter in her hands.

Angel Talk

*T*hey like each other!" The Little Angel of Friendship ran like mad, took a giant leap, and tumbled to a stop.

The Archangel of Friendship looked at him in astonishment.

"It's a broad jump," said the little angel. "I'm practicing for the angel talent show next month."

"Oh. Well, that's an impressive jump."

"Yup. And even though my wings will be fully feathered, I won't use them to help at all."

The archangel raised an eyebrow. "Isn't that called 'counting your chickens before they're hatched'? You haven't earned those wings yet."

"But they like each other. You saw. And he's a much better friend than those snotty girls."

The archangel put a hand over her mouth,

but the little angel could see she was hiding a smile. "You're a bit quick on judging people as not being worthy of friendship, don't you think?"

"No. Lynsey just walked past Patricia as though she were a piece of wood or something. She didn't even wave."

"Maybe she's worried about how to deal with Patricia. After all, that experience together wasn't good for her, either."

"Maybe," said the little angel grudgingly. "Anyway, Patricia has a friend in that boy, so I'm earning my wings, that's for sure."

"I like your enthusiasm, but slow down. Would you be satisfied with a friend you could only squirt water guns with and roll around in a garbage can?"

"They can play ball, too," said the little angel.

"Yes, but is that enough?"

"Sure."

"Really?" asked the archangel. "Wouldn't you want to tell your friend all the things that were on your mind?"

"No."

"That sounds like a pretty odd idea of friendship," said the Archangel of Friendship.

"That's how lots of guys do it. Anyway, I thought you were the one who said she could make friends through actions. Now you're changing what you said."

"Not exactly," said the archangel. "People can learn a lot about each other by doing things together. But language is the way we share our thoughts and hopes and dreams. It's much harder to do that without language."

"Then Patricia is in terrible trouble, because she doesn't speak."

"She has a language, though." The archangel smiled. "A perfectly good one."

"Oh." The little angel slowly brightened. "Oh," he said louder. "Patricia can't hear, but that boy can see—and he can move his hands. I'm getting an idea."

"I thought you might."

Tank

On Saturday morning, Mom woke Patricia up to tell her that someone had come to see her.

"Who?"

But Mom just turned around and went into the living room.

Patricia put on her clothes fast and ran into the living room. The boy was there. Patricia looked past him all around the room, but Lynsey was nowhere to be found.

The boy smiled at her and handed her an index card.

Patricia read it. It said, "I'm Edward, but I like people to call me Tank."

Without thinking, Patricia raised her eyebrows and made the sign for an army tank. Then she caught herself.

But Tank didn't laugh at the sign. He

looked confused. He shrugged and pointed to the table. A two hundred-piece puzzle box sat there. He went over and dumped out all the pieces.

Patricia was good at puzzles. She looked at the picture on the box. A spaceship scene.

Tank was already organizing the pieces, putting all the edge pieces to one side and arranging the others by color.

Patricia tapped his arm.

Tank looked up.

Suddenly Patricia didn't know what to do. She wanted to let him know that she had to eat and brush her teeth before she could do the puzzle with him. But how? She stood there.

Tank looked at her and cocked his head. Then he went back to work on the puzzle.

Patricia went to the bathroom and brushed her teeth. Next she scooted into the kitchen and poured herself a bowl of cereal. She glanced over the counter into the living room. Tank examined the puzzle pieces with total concentration. Patricia was delighted with this turn of events. She'd thought he only liked sports. But maybe he liked lots of things. The brown-spotted bananas in the basket on the counter smelled strong. Patricia cut one into her cereal. Then she added milk and carried the bowl back to the table.

Tank looked wistfully at her cereal.

Patricia ran back to the kitchen and got another bowl. She held up two boxes of cereal for Tank to choose: Cheerios and Honey Bunches of Oats.

Tank shook his head. He pointed to the cereal in Patricia's bowl.

Patricia smiled and shook the Cheerios box.

Tank shook his head again. He pointed more vigorously to Patricia's cereal bowl.

From nowhere came a little wind, and it carried with it the heavy scent of the ripe bananas. There was banana in Patricia's cereal. Maybe that's what Tank was pointing at? Patricia reached for the fruit basket. And now the wind was strong on her face, blowing in her eyes. She had to stop and close them for a second. When she opened them, she could see Tank looking at her intensely. It was almost as though he was studying her.

Patricia slowly held her left index finger up and motioned peeling it with her right hand. That was the sign for "banana." Her cheeks went hot. She kept her eyes on Tank's eyes as she signed, "Banana," again.

Tank looked at her hand. A smile of recognition burst onto his face. He held up his own index finger and copied Patricia.

She brought him a banana.

Tank laughed. Then his face lit up. He tapped her bowl.

Patricia made the sign for "bowl."

Tank copied it. He tapped the table. Then he copied her making the sign. They went all around the room together, with Patricia making the signs for everything Tank pointed at and Tank copying her.

All at once Tank stopped and grabbed Patricia by the arm. He pointed at himself urgently.

"What?" Patricia shook her head. "You? You just point to yourself to mean you."

Tank reached in his pocket and took out the card he'd shown Patricia earlier, the one that told his name. Then he pointed at himself again.

"Oh!" Patricia made the sign for "tank."

Tank copied her, then pointed to himself. He'd given himself a sign name.

Dad laughed, Mom laughed, Tank laughed, and Patricia—she laughed and laughed.

Angel Talk

He's a quick learner," said the Archangel of Friendship.

"I knew he was a terrific guy," said the little angel. "He's a thousand times better than his sister. He loves learning sign language."

"Hold on a minute. Lynsey could still be a nice person."

"Well, it doesn't matter," said the little angel, "because Patricia is friends with Tank."

"Are you saying they can't both be friends with Patricia?"

"If I had to choose between them, I'd choose Tank," said the little angel.

"Does Patricia have to choose between them?"

"Aw, come on," said the little angel. "Lynsey decided she didn't like Patricia."

"Maybe. Tell me, little angel, when you first saw Tank, exercising with his barbells in front of the TV, did you expect Patricia to become friends with him?"

"No." The little angel squatted and put his head on the ground. Slowly he extended his legs above him till he was in a full headstand. He grinned at the archangel. "But the moment I saw him upside down, I knew I liked him. He's nice."

"He can do mean things. He cut all the hair off Lynsey's doll."

"So that's why it was bald. I wondered." The little angel wiggled his toes over his head. "I guess that was pretty mean."

"The first time you saw Lynsey, did you think she was nice? Did you think she'd become friends with Patricia?" The archangel tickled the little angel's feet.

The Little Angel of Friendship laughed. "Yes." He lowered his legs and did three somer-saults in a row. "Lynsey wanted to make friends with Patricia. She didn't care that Patricia was deaf. I liked her at first."

"So what do you think happened? Really? Why did Lynsey change?"

The little angel looked at the archangel. "I see what you're getting at. Tank's an adventuresome person. Maybe Lynsey isn't. Maybe she can't figure out how to begin making friends with Patricia."

"I was just thinking that, too," said the archangel.

The little angel remembered how bad Patricia had felt when Lynsey walked past her out by the Dumpster last night. Patricia wanted to be friends with Lynsey. "And maybe Patricia doesn't know how to help her. I guess my job's not over yet."

Three Together

Patricia crept behind Tank down the long apartment hallway. She moved her paws slowly and stealthily. They were panthers.

When they reached the end of the hall, Tank signed, "You choose, now." It was one of about a dozen sentences he knew how to sign already.

"Let's be goats."

Tank narrowed his eyes. He didn't know this sign.

Patricia kicked her heels like Nanny. She butted Tank in the shoulder. She stood splay-legged.

Still, Tank couldn't figure out what she was. He took out the pad of paper and pencil that he'd run home to get earlier and handed them to Patricia.

She wrote, "Goats," and signed it again.

Tank mimicked her. He grinned. He obviously liked goats.

Patricia made the sign for "wait." She ran back to her apartment and dashed into her bedroom. The third box still stood in the corner. Patricia lifted the flaps. She grabbed the quarter bale of hay by the strings around it and heaved it onto the floor, then shoved it under her bed. Tonight she'd dream she was sleeping in a barn. She took the pile of ash leaves, which were now half brown and limp, and strewed them along her windowsill. Under the last handful of leaves was what she was searching for: Nanny's bell. Patricia ran with it back to the hall. She tied it around Tank's neck.

Tank puffed out his chest proudly. Then he looked past Patricia.

Patricia turned around.

Lynsey stood there. She moved her mouth at Tank.

Tank moved his mouth back.

Lynsey looked at Patricia solemnly. She moved her mouth again.

Tank signed, "Goat," to Lynsey.

Lynsey's eyes grew sad. Her nose turned red.

A wind blew in Patricia's face. It blew so hard, tears came to her eyes. In an instant, she understood that Lynsey felt like crying. Lynsey felt left out. Patricia touched Lynsey softly on the arm. She made the sign for "goat." Then she took the pad of paper from Tank and showed Lynsey the word she'd written.

Lynsey nodded.

Patricia made the sign for "goat" again.

Lynsey pursed her lips. Then she signed, "Goat."

Patricia smiled. She wrote, "We're playing goats."

Lynsey nodded.

Tank lowered his head and charged them both.

Angel Thoughts

The newest archangel of friendship flew all around the heavens. He could still hear the goat bell ringing, as Tank and Lynsey and Patricia jumped around and butted each other. It was a great sound—the sound that heralded his earning his wings. But he couldn't stay to listen to it for long, because he had someone to find. A little angel who scribbled on a pad of paper all the time and only said, "Yo." That little angel just might be a friend, given a chance. The newest archangel of friendship didn't know, but he sure was going to find out.

American Sign
Language Alphabet

Meet the Little Angel of Freedom in the next 𝒜𝓃𝑔𝑒𝓁𝓌𝒾𝓃𝑔𝓈

№. 2 Little Creatures

The Little Angel of Freedom held a nectar-dipped fingertip out to the butterfly that clung to her shoulder. The butterfly sipped daintily. "Is this the house?" the little angel asked. "I don't see anyone."

"Wait," said the Archangel of Freedom. He pointed.

A girl came into the kitchen and tapped the glass jar on the table. The grasshopper inside the jar jumped. "Are you still hungry?" The girl ran out the back door and ripped a handful of grass from the yard. Then she poked the blades one by one through the holes in the jar lid. They fell soft on the grasshopper's head.

"The grasshopper needs to get out," said the Archangel of Freedom.

The little angel frowned. "The girl has made sure he can breathe. And she's feeding him well." She looked at her own pet butterfly and nodded. "I think she's taking good care of him."

The girl tapped the jar again. The grasshopper jumped, but this time not so high. "Good night. Sleep tight." She ran off.

The Archangel of Freedom pointed out the window. "Yesterday, before he was caught, this grasshopper jumped from the edge of the porch up to the first crook of that peach tree." He looked at the little angel. "If you could jump that high and that far, would you be happy in a jar?"

The Little Angel of Freedom folded her hands together. She didn't look at the archangel.

A woman came into the kitchen. She picked up the jar and carried it outside. She stooped in the yard and unscrewed the lid.

The grasshopper just sat in the bottom of the jar.

The woman tilted the jar till the grasshopper slid out into the grass. He stayed there a moment, looking stunned. Then he jumped away.

"Whenever the girl catches something, the mother has to come down at night and set it free."

"Well, then, it's no problem at all," said the little angel.

"Sometimes the creature gets injured, bashing itself against the side of the jar." The Archangel of Freedom's voice was quiet and gentle. "Sometimes it even dies before the mother can set it free."

"Oh." The Little Angel of Freedom watched the grasshopper stop and chew on a leaf.

"Your wings are about halfway feathered. You've done a good job earning those feathers." The Archangel of Freedom smiled. "I'm proud of all your deeds."

"It's been hard. Every feather is so hard to earn." The little angel put her hand in her left pocket and wiggled her fingers in the soft pile of ground black pepper she kept there. Pepper was her secret tool. In her right pocket she kept a small pool of flower nectar for her butterfly. She felt fully equipped.

"Well," said the Archangel, "now you have a chance to earn the rest of your feathers."

"All of them?" The little angel brushed her hands together to clean off the pepper. Then she stroked her thinly feathered wings. "All of them at once?"

"Not really at once. Our little girl, Simone, needs lots of help. For each time you help her, you'll earn a feather. She's quite a problem. I bet you'll earn your wings on this one."

Her wings. When a little angel earns her last feather, she really earns her wings, because then she can fly, like all the archangels. The little angel shivered at the thought. A bell rings when an angel earns her wings. What kind of bell would the Little Angel of Freedom hear?

Don't miss these other
Aladdin *Angelwings* stories:

№.2 Little Creatures

№.3 On Her Own

Coming soon!
№.4 One Leap Forward

Earn Your Wings! essay contest

Win

＊ A $250 Gap gift certificate

＊ Your name in an Aladdin Angelwings book

＊ $100 worth of Simon & Schuster
Children's books

＊ $250 worth of Simon & Schuster Children's
books donated to your school's library

＊　　＊　　＊

Describe your good deed in
300 words or less for your
chance to win.

Have you earned your
Angelwings?

Official Rules
Aladdin Angelwings
"Earn Your Wings" Contest

1. No purchase necessary. Submission must include one original essay on the good deed you have done (not to exceed 300 words). Entries should be typed (preferable) or printed legibly. Mail your essay to: Simon & Schuster Children's Publishing Division, Marketing Department, Aladdin Angelwings "Earn Your Wings" Contest, 1230 Avenue of the Americas, New York, New York 10020. Each essay can only be entered once. Contest begins September 15, 1999. Entries must be received by December 31, 1999. Not responsible for postage due, late, lost, stolen, damaged, incomplete, not delivered, mutilated, illegible, or misdirected entries, or for typographical errors in the rules. Entries are void if they are in whole or in part illegible, incomplete, or damaged. Enter as often as you wish, but each entry must be different and mailed separately. Essays will be judged by Simon & Schuster Children's Publishing on the following basis: 80% good deed done, 20% writing ability. All entries must be original and the sole property of the entrant. Entries must not have been previously published or have won any awards. All submissions become the property of Simon & Schuster and will not be returned. By entering, entrants agree to abide by these rules. Void where prohibited by law.

2. Winner will be selected from a judging of all eligible entries received and will be announced on or about March 1, 2000. Selected entrant will be notified by mail.

3. One Consumer Grand Prize: The winner will receive a $250 gift certificate at Gap Clothing Stores, $100 worth of Simon & Schuster Children's Publishing books, have $250 worth of Simon & Schuster Children's Publishing books donated to his or her school's library, and have his or her name appear in a future Aladdin Angelwings book. The winner's essay may appear in future publication(s) from Simon & Schuster or advertising for the Aladdin Angelwings series.

4. Contest is open to legal residents of U.S. and Canada (excluding Quebec). Winner must be 14 years of age or younger as of December 31, 1999. Employees and immediate family members (or those with which they are domiciled) of Simon & Schuster, its parent, subsidiaries, divisions, and related companies and their respective agencies and agents are ineligible. Prize will be awarded to the winner's parent or legal guardian.

5. Prize is not transferable and may not be substituted except by Simon & Schuster. In the event of prize unavailability, a prize of equal or greater value will be awarded.

6. All expenses on receipt of prize, including federal, state, provincial and local taxes, are the sole responsibility of the winner. Winner's legal guardian will be required to execute and return an Affidavit of Eligibility and Release and all other legal documents that Simon & Schuster may require (including but not limited to an assignment to Simon & Schuster of all rights including copyright in and to the winning essay and the exclusive right of Simon & Schuster to publish the winning entry in any form or media) within 15 days of attempted notification or an alternate winner will be selected.

7. By accepting a prize, winner grants to Simon & Schuster the right to use his/her entry and name and likeness for any advertising, promotional, trade, or any other purpose without further compensation or permission, except where prohibited by law.

8. Simon & Schuster shall have no liability for any injury, loss, or damage of any kind, arising out of participation in this contest or the acceptance or use of a prize.

9. The winner's first name and home state or province, available after 3/15/00, may be obtained by sending a separate, stamped, self-addressed envelope to: Winner's List, Aladdin Angelwings "Earn Your Wings" Contest, Simon & Schuster Children's Marketing Department, 1230 Avenue of the Americas, New York, NY 10020.